THE ALPHABET FROM A TO Z (WITH MUCH CONFUSION ON THE WAY)

BY

JUDITH VIORST

ILLUSTRATED BY RICHARD HULL

ATHENEUM · 1994 · NEW YORK

Maxwell Macmillan Canada
TORONTO

Maxwell Macmillan International
NEW YORK   OXFORD   SINGAPORE   SYDNEY

Atheneum
Macmillan Publishing Company
866 Third Avenue
New York, NY 10022

Maxwell Macmillan Canada, Inc.
1200 Eglinton Avenue East
Suite 200
Don Mills, Ontario M3C 3N1

Macmillan Publishing Company is part of
the Maxwell Communication Group of Companies.

First edition
Printed in the United States of America

10   9   8   7   6   5   4   3   2   1

The text of this book is set in 15-point Weiss.
The illustrations are rendered in acrylic paints.

Library of Congress Cataloging-in-Publication Data

Viorst, Judith.
    The Alphabet from Z to A: (with much confusion on the way) / by
Judith Viorst; illustrated by Richard Hull. —1st ed.
        p.   cm.
    Summary: Verses running backwards through the alphabet take note
of some anomalies in English spelling and pronunciation.
    ISBN 0-689-31768-9
    1. English language—Alphabet—Juvenile poetry.   2. Children's
poetry, American.   3. Alphabet rhymes.   [1. English language—
Poetry.   2. American poetry.   3. Alphabet.]   i. Hull, Richard,
1945–   ill.   II. Title.
PS3572.I6A79   1994
E—dc20
[811'.54]   91–39338

is for ZIP, ZAP, and ZERO.
But XYLOPHONE doesn't
(Why not?) start with Z.

is for *YEW* and for *YOU*,

But it isn't for *USING*.

is for *X-RAY* and *EXCELLENT*.
Hold it right there!
What's the matter with me?
EXCELLENT starts with an *E*,
Not an *X*.
It's confusing!

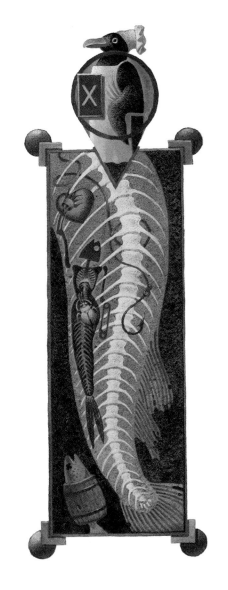

must be for *WHO*,

But it isn't for *HOOT*.

Don't you think that's a pain?

W's also for *WHICH, WITCH,*

WHY, WIDE, WERE, and *WORRY*.

is for *VALE* and for *VEIL*,

And (I cannot believe this!)

For *VANE, VAIN,* and *VEIN*!

R is for—we're not at *R* yet.

Now, what is your hurry?

is for *UNDERWEAR,*
UNCLE, UNWRAP,
But it can't be for *ONION.*
Absurd!

is for *TAXI* and *TACKS*,
TRAY, and *TRACE*,
TWO, TOO, TO. This
Isn't the worst. *T*'s for *TURKEY*,
But back in the dinosaur days lived a bird
Named—help!—*PTERODACTYL*.
What in the world makes folks *do* this?

is for *SURE* and for *SHORE*,
And for *SUN* and for *SEA*,
And for *SEE* and for *SON*.

is for *RING, RANG,* and *RUNG,*

And yet *RONG* would be wrong, dear.

is for *QUEUE*, but not *CUE*.

And for one *QUIET QUESTION*:

Are we almost done?

Answer: There're sixteen more letters

Still left in this song, dear.

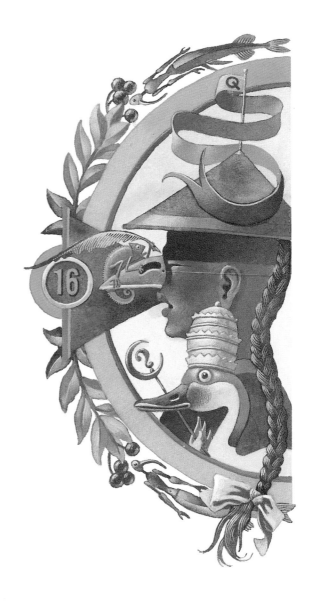

is for *PHONE, PHILODENDRON,*

And *PHYSICAL* fitness,

Which only counts half.

Wish we could spell the word *PHITNESS,*

But they won't permit it.

is for *OR, ORE,* and *ORANGES.*

Also *ORANGUTANS.*

This is a laugh!

is for *NIT, NIGHT,* and *NOT,* but not
KNOT, KNIGHT, or *KNIT.* It
'S also for *NOW* (but not *GNAW*)
And for *NOME* (in Alaska)
But not (darn!) for *GNOME.*

is for *MIST, MISSED, MY, MINE.*

Now my mind is a muddle.

is for *LAY, LEI,* and *LACE,*
And it also meant fifty
In long-ago Rome.

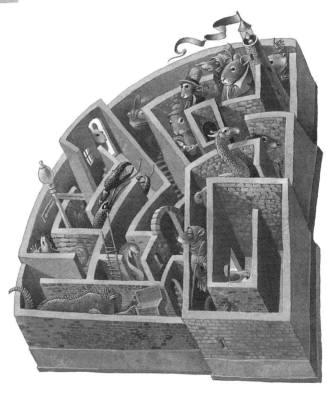

is for *KISS*,
But they won't let us use it
For *CUDDLE*.

is for *JEWEL* but not *GEM*.

It cannot be for *GENIUS,*

But can be for *JERK*.

is for *IN* and for *INN*,

And I ought to be saying

I is for *I*

(But not *EYE*)

And for *ISLE*

(But not *AISLE*).

It could drive you berserk.

Let's take a break and make
H just for *HIP-HIP-HOORAYING*.

is for GO and for *GHOST*.

It's for *GULL* and for *GEL*.

It's for *GEE* but not *JEEP*.

is for *FAKE* but not *PHONY*.

That should be unlawful.

is for *EVE* and for *EVER,*
For *EAR* and for *EARLY.*
I'm going to weep.

is for *DEW, DO,*

DYE, DIE,

DOE, DOUGH.

Isn't it awful?

is for CEILING and CHUTE,

But we aren't to use it

For SEAL or for SHOE.

is for *BOUGH, BOW, BLEW, BLUE.*

No, it doesn't get better.

Ah, but here's A for *ASTONISHED*

That somehow I've managed

To rhyme my way through

To the last—whoops! excuse me!

I mean the *first*—alphabet letter.

A Challenge

The illustrations for each of the letters in this book are full of objects—plants and animals and people and things—whose names start with that letter. Though most of these objects are easy to find (*zebra* for Z, for instance), several are only medium easy, some are really quite hard, and a few of them are *totally* impossible. (Blame Richard Hull, who drew them. Don't blame me.) We invite you to go back and see how many objects you can find and name, and then compare your list with our list. Remember that each illustration includes some objects that do *not* start with that letter. Don't be tricked into putting them on your list.

JUDITH VIORST

P.S. You might even find a few objects that Richard and I forgot to mention. Hey, we're not perfect.

Our List

Z

zebra, zero, zinnia, zipper

Y

yacht, yak, yellowbird, (aka goldfinch or yellow warbler), yellow jacket, yellow perch, yeoman, yew, yucca, yule (as in Christmas, represented here by a Christmas bulb)

X

(These are, we admit, our most outrageous words.)
xanthine and xanthin (parts of the yellow coloring matter in flowers), xerophyte (a desert plant), Xiphosura (a zoological order made up of king crabs), X-marks-the-spot (not totally fair, but fair enough), X ray, xylem (the woody tissue of a plant)

W

wand, wave, weevil, wheat, whiskers, wings, witch, worm

V

valentine, vampire, vane, vase, veil, Venus, vermin (that's what the mouse is), Viking, vine, violet, viper (that's what the snake is), vulture

U

ukulele, umbrella, uncle (as in surrendering and waving the white flag), underwear, ungulates (mammals that have hooves—the ram, for instance), unicorn, urn

T

tadpoles, target, teardrop, tepee, thorns, tie, tiger, tracks, train, tree, triangle, trumpet vine, tulips, turkey, turtle, tuxedo, two

S

sailboats, sailor boy (in sailor suit), sardines, saw, scallop, sea, sea horse, seal, seashell, seaweed, snail, snorkel, sombrero, square, square knot, starfish, stars, submarine, sun, sunfish, sunglasses

R

rabbit, raccoon, raspberries, rat, rattlesnake (or reptile), raven (the only *red* raven in existence), rhinoceros, ribbon, ring, roach (a kind of fish), rooster, rose, rowboat, rungs

Q

quail, queen, question mark, quetzal (no, we didn't make this one up—it's a crested bird of Central America), queue, quill pen, quilt

P

panda, parking meter, parrot, peacock, pear, pelican, pen, penguin, perch, periscope, periwinkle (a snail, for instance), pharaoh, philodendron, phone, piano keys, pig, pilgrim, pillar, plunger, primate (a gorilla, for instance), puffer fish, punctuation mark (it's an exclamation point!), python

O

oar, ocean, o'clock (this doesn't really count, but we couldn't resist), octopus, *oculus* (an eye), oil lamp, olive, olive drab (that's what they call a soldier's uniform), opah (a large sea fish, though probably not one you've ever heard of), oranges, orangutan, ostrich, otter, outboard motor, oval, ovine (a sheeplike animal), owl, ox

N

nail, necktie, needlefish, needles (for knitting), newt, night, night crawlers, nighthawk, nine, nit (a young louse), North Star (that's the star the Big Dipper points to), nose

M

maiden, man (in mouse mask, maybe marrying maiden), mandolin, milkweed, monkey, moon, moth, mouse (or if you wish, mouse musician or even—do you believe this?—mouse mermaid), mouth, muses (making music)

L

L (equals 50), labyrinth, lace, ladder, ladybugs, lamp, lamprey (an eellike water animal—you'll find it sweating in the labyrinth, probably because it wishes it were back in the water), laying hen, leaping lake trout, legionnaire (or close enough), lei, lighthouse, lion, lizard, llama, lobster, lovebird, lupines (a kind of plant)

K

kangaroo, katydid, kayak, keep, key, kid, king, king cobra, kingfisher, king snake, kiss, kite, kittens, knight (with kyphosis—a humpback), knitting yarn

J

jack-in-the-box (with juggling jester in a jacket), jack-o'-lantern, jackrabbit, jaguar, jail, jets, jewels, joey (a baby kangaroo), junco (aka finch), jungle, Jupiter

I

ibex (a wild goat), ibis (a long-legged wading bird), ice-cream cone, ichthyopsid (sorry about this, but it means a member of the zoological classification that includes fish), igloo, iguana, inchworm (actually a worm with a bird's head—no, we're not kidding), Indian, inner tube, insect, iris (the eye kind and the flower kind), island

H

half-moon, halibut, hands, hare, harness, hat, headset, hedgehog, hemispheres (if a hemisphere is half a globe, then two hemispheres make a whole globe, right?), hen, heron, hexagons (these are six-sided figures—take another look at the honeycomb), hibiscus, hive, hobbyhorse, honeybee, honeycomb

G

galleon, gargoyle, garter snake, geraniums, ghost, globe, goldfish, golf ball, grass, gull

F

face, fairy, feathers, feet, feline, female fortune-teller, figs, fingers, fins, fish (flying and otherwise), fleur-de-lis, flowers, flute, fly, fool, fowl, frog, funnel

E

eagle, eardrum (sorry about that), earring, ears, earth, Easter eggs, eel, eider (a large sea duck), elephant, elf, ellipse, Eve (in Eden), evening, eyeglasses, eyes

D

daffodils, daisies, dart, dart board, dawn, deer, dewdrops, diamonds, dinnerware, dinosaur, dodo, doe (in damsel's dress), dog (hot and dachshund), dots (a dozen of them), dough, dragonfly, duck (diving or dying?), dwarf

C

cactus, candle, cane, cap, cat, catfish, ceiling, chair, checkers, cherubs, chicken, chute, circles, clock, cobra, cod, collar, columns, comet, cone, cowboy hat, crane, crocuses, crown, curtain

B

bagpipe, banner, beard, bees, bells, berry, birds, bird's nest, bluebells, boa, boot, bow, branches, brick, bucket, bugle, bugs, bull's-eyes, butterfly

A

alligator, aloe, angel wings, angler, angleworm, ant, anteater, antelope, antennae, apple, arbor (that group of trees), archer, armor, arms, arrow, astral bodies (stars), ax